Tom and Pippo in the Garden,
Tom and Pippo Go Shopping and
Tom and Pippo Go for a Walk first published 1988
Tom and Pippo Make a Friend,
Tom and Pippo and the Dog and
Tom and Pippo in the Snow first published 1989
by Walker Books Ltd, 87 Vauxhall Walk, London SE11 5HJ

This edition published 1995

10 9 8 7 6 5 4 3 2 1

© 1988, 1989 Helen Oxenbury

This book has been typeset in Stempel Schneidler Medium.

Printed in Hong Kong

British Library Cataloguing in Publication Data
A catalogue record for this book is
available from the British Library.

ISBN 0-7445-3775-4 (hb)
ISBN 0-7445-3720-7 (pb)

SIX TODDLER STORIES

Out
and
About
with
TOM
AND
PIPPO

Helen Oxenbury

WALKER BOOKS
AND SUBSIDIARIES
LONDON · BOSTON · SYDNEY

Tom
and
Pippo
in the
Garden

I often take Pippo
into the garden.
He likes to ride in my
wheelbarrow.

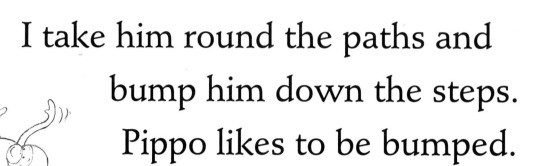

I take him round the paths and
bump him down the steps.
Pippo likes to be bumped.
When we've had enough, I give
him his dinner. Pippo
makes a mess when
he eats. He gets
food all over his face.
So I have to wipe
him with a flannel.

When I hear Mummy calling,
I make a little bed for Pippo
so he can sleep while I eat
my lunch.
After lunch,
when we
want to play, that cat
is asleep in my
wheelbarrow. We
have to shoo him out.

Then I take Pippo
round and round
the garden until
it is time to go
in for tea.

Tom and Pippo Make a Friend

One day Mummy took me to the place where you can play in the sandpit and I found a lovely bucket.

I was just making castles with the
bucket when this little girl
came and tried
to take
it away
from me.
She said it
was her
bucket.

The little girl's mummy said
we should share our toys.
But Pippo is mine.
I really wanted to play with that bucket,
and Pippo wanted
to play with
it too. So we
all played
together in
the sandpit.

Today we're
going to the
sandpit again.
I hope the little
girl is there with
her bucket.

Tom and Pippo and the Dog

I went for a walk with Mummy, and we met a friend with her dog. I was just having a game with Pippo, when along came the dog.

The dog wanted to play with us, I could tell. I wasn't doing anything. Then suddenly the  dog snatched Pippo.

"My monkey's gone," I shouted. We all ran after the dog. But he ran very quickly.

16

I thought we would never catch him and Pippo would be gone for ever. The lady caught the dog and was cross with him. I was glad to have Pippo back.

I think Pippo
really might
have liked being
carried off by
the dog.

Tom and Pippo in the Snow

One morning it had snowed really hard.  Daddy bought a sledge and said we should take it up the hill. I took Pippo because he wanted to come. We had never been on a sledge before.

We took the sledge up the hill. I thought Pippo would like to have first go. Daddy said there was nothing to be frightened of. But I said it was only fair to let Pippo go on the sledge first. I could tell he wanted to.

So Daddy brought Pippo to the top of the hill and I waited at the bottom. Daddy said, "If Pippo can do it, I'm sure you can too."

I said to Daddy, "Why don't we all go on the sledge?" Daddy said the sledge was really too small. So in the end I went all by myself.

Going on a sledge
is really very easy.
Pippo and I go by
ourselves all the
time. We don't
need Daddy.

Tom and Pippo Go Shopping

Today
Mummy and
I went shopping.
I took Pippo. Pippo likes
to go to the shops.

I said he would love a little piece of bread. But I ate it. I said Pippo would love a ripe, juicy plum. But I ate it. Pippo wanted just a little piece of cheese from the cheese counter. But I ate it.

When we had bought all the shopping,
Mummy gave me the money
and said I could pay.
Mummy had
a cup of tea
and I had a
little drink.
But there
wasn't enough
for Pippo.

Anyway,
I'll give Pippo
some tea when
we get home.

Tom and Pippo Go for a Walk

Mummy and I were going for a walk. Mummy said it was very cold outside and I must wear my hat, scarf and gloves.

Pippo wanted to come for
a walk too. I made him put
on his hat and scarf
and I told him he
would catch a cold
if he didn't.
Mummy held
Pippo while
I went for a run
down the hill.

Pippo wanted to run
with me, but we fell over.
I'm sure Pippo made
me run too fast.

Mummy put me
straight in the
bath, but Pippo
had to go in
the basin.

Then Pippo and
I sat by the fire
and had a
warm drink.